# In Your Heart Lives a Rainbow

*To our beloved parents*
*Joan and Jerry*
*who were our inspiration*
*for the book series*

D1088580

**Story and Songs**
**by Karen Seader**

**Illustrations**
**by Valerie Lynn**

In Your Heart Lives a Rainbow, LLC

Published by **In Your Heart Lives a Rainbow, LLC**

ISBN: 978-0-9857824-0-5

Library of Congress Catalog Card Number: 2013917964

Manufactured by Color House Graphics, Inc., Grand Rapids, MI, USA  Job# 42412, March 2014

Music and Lyrics Copyright ©2006 by Karen Seader
Musical Arrangements by Larry Sacchetillo

Book 1 includes CD of 11 songs for the first three books of the series.
Song tracks correspond to the illustrated song pages in each book.
The songs can also be downloaded from our website:
**InYourHeartLivesaRainbow.com**

Karen Seader - author, singer, and songwriter, along with her sister Valerie Lynn - illustrator, co-created the **In Your Heart Lives a Rainbow**® book series with original songs. Combining fantasy and reality, this dynamic, innovative series focuses on character building and positive life skills to make a significant difference in children's lives.

"Our goal is to reach and empower children, families, and educators, to be a motivating and nurturing force that **brings out the best in children** and **brings Love and Unity into the world**."

BOOK 1 - *In Your Heart Lives a Rainbow*
Hailey and Logan (big sister and brother) are delighted to meet The Lady of the Rainbow in a magical dream. Inspired by her message and songs, upon awakening, a series of events occur where the children discover the power of smiling, being kind, and believing in yourself.

**Karen Seader** is the co-creator and the author, singer/songwriter of the **In Your Heart Lives a Rainbow**® book series.

She embodies **The Lady of the Rainbow**®, the magical character who inspires and motivates the children. Karen has used the medium of entertainment for more than 20 years to work with over 50,000 children in interactive shows performed at schools, libraries, organizations, camps, parties, and community events. "I truly love connecting with children as **The Lady of the Rainbow**® and creating joyous and meaningful events! I see how receptive they are to the positive, uplifting concepts that are offered in the stories and songs."

**Valerie Lynn** is the co-creator and illustrator of the **In Your Heart Lives a Rainbow**® book series.

She designed the costume for the **The Lady of the Rainbow**® live show, as well as created the trademarked character. Valerie is a professional fine artist, exhibiting throughout the Northeast. She is a graduate of Parsons School of Design and created her own unique line of fashion artwear, which sold nationally and internationally in fine department stores and boutiques around the world.

Snuggled in their nice cozy beds, Hailey and Logan said "Good night" to each other and closed their eyes. They didn't know that this was going to be a very special night!

Suddenly, brightly colored lights appeared before them!
Gazing into the middle of the lights, they began spiraling upward...

...lifted and carried by a magical rainbow!
Laughing with delight, they flew higher and higher!!

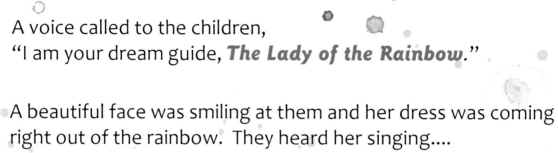

A voice called to the children,
"I am your dream guide, *The Lady of the Rainbow*."

A beautiful face was smiling at them and her dress was coming right out of the rainbow. They heard her singing....

Smile and See
Just What a Smile Can Bring
Like the Sunshine
Its Warmth Keeps Echoing

Flowers Need
The Raindrops From Above
And Our Hearts
Blossom With Love

"Why did you come to us?" asked the children.

"To let you and everyone know that
IN YOUR HEART LIVES A RAINBOW.

It's up to each of us to let it shine as bright as we can!"

The children pointed to something
shimmering in the sky.

"Look, it's a Rainbow Fairy!" they exclaimed.

"Hi, my name is Jilly," she said
in a cheerful voice.

*The Lady of the Rainbow* explained
"Jilly is my special helper."

"And I'm going to be your special friend,"
Jilly added.

"I'll be here to help you remember
all the wonderful things you learn
from *The Lady of the Rainbow*."

"Will everyone see you?" asked Logan.

"Sometimes they will and sometimes they won't," giggled Jilly.

"You'll have to look closely to find me.
I like flying quickly!
I like dancing and twirling and whirling
and even flying upside down!

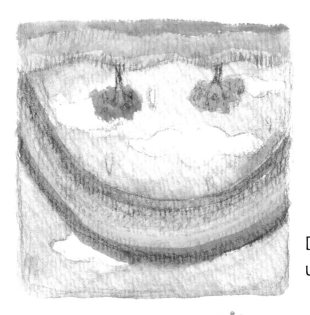

Did you know that when you look at a rainbow
upside down, it looks like the whole sky is smiling?!

Hailey and Logan danced
with the *The Lady of the Rainbow* while
Jilly whizzed around twirling on their heads,
making them all laugh!

# Everybody loves when

Everybody loves
When someone's smiling
It brightens up the day
And night time too

Everybody loves
When someone's smiling
Oh why
Oh why wouldn't you?

When you wake up
You see the sun is smiling
The flowers smile
All afternoon

Before going to bed
Look out the window
There's a shining smile
On the moon

# someone's smiling

Everybody loves
When someone's smiling
It brightens up the day
And **night time** too
Everybody loves
When someone's smiling
Oh why
Oh why wouldn't you?

When we're kind to each other
And we're loving
We brighten up the day
And **night time** too
We fill the world
With love and beauty
And find
The world is **smiling** too

*The Lady of the Rainbow* waved goodbye to the children. Brilliant colors flowed from her hands, encircling them in a warm embrace. They smiled as they heard her singing...

## A Golden Opportunity

All through your lives
You will see
A golden opportunity

A chance for you to be
The very best
That you can be

The next morning Hailey and Logan
woke up in very cheerful moods.  Even though it was raining, their smiles
filled the room with warm sunlight.

They hurried downstairs to breakfast and gave Mommy and Daddy extra big good morning hugs.
Mommy said, "I wasn't feeling well when I woke up, but your smiling faces and hugs make me feel much better!"

At school Hailey heard some children tell Sophie that they didn't want to play with her.

Hailey felt bad, but didn't know what to do, so she continued coloring with her friend Zabi.

Suddenly, JILLY the RAINBOW FAIRY appeared twirling and whirling on top of Sophie's head! That made Hailey smile.

Sophie thought Hailey was smiling at her. That made her smile back.

While smiling at each other, Hailey again felt warm sunlight filling the room, even though it was still raining outside.

She thought, "It's very easy to ask Sophie to play with us," and that's what she did.

The teacher noticed all the children having fun! Now she had a big smile on her face.

In Logan's classroom Show 'n Tell was about to begin.
The day before the teacher had written on the blackboard,

BRING IN SOMETHING COLORFUL

Logan could hardly sit still.  He was so excited to
surprise the class with what he had in his pocket.

Waiting for his turn, Logan's friend Dylan sadly said,
"I don't have anything to show.  I left it at home."

The teacher exclaimed, "But Dylan you did bring something
colorful...a rainbow!"

Dylan looked down at his white T-shirt,
and with a big smile on his face he said,
"How did that get there?"

Logan had taken the little object out of his pocket, and with a
grin from ear to ear, proudly announced, "it's my prism!"

He moved it around while the delighted children pointed
to the little rainbows appearing all over the room.

The teacher explained, "A prism is a special object that can catch light
and bounce it off itself, creating the 7 colors of the rainbow...
But what's more special is that Logan used it to make someone smile!"

Walking home from school, Hailey and Logan got caught in a storm.

Rain poured down on their heads and gusts of wind blew leaves in their faces!

Logan began to cry.
Hailey was frightened, because they couldn't see the pathway home anymore.

Hailey pointed, "Let's go under that tree."

Nestled against the big, old tree,
the children felt safe and protected.

Logan whispered, "Don't these branches
feel a little like Daddy hugging us?"

They fell asleep with the soft leaves
embracing them.

They dreamt that a long branch was lifting them up.
They were amazed that the tree had a face and
he was smiling!

They looked up and saw the beautiful *Lady of the Rainbow*.
She said, "I want to introduce you to my dear friend
**FATHER TREE**. He has been sheltering you from the storm."

"Thank you **FATHER TREE**," the children said.

In a deep voice the tree replied, "I'm very happy I could help you. Jilly told me that you also helped your friends today. If you keep doing kind things you are going to be very special people."

"But we're just little kids!" exclaimed Logan.

**The Lady of the Rainbow** smiled and said, "Well, let me tell you about my good friend **FATHER TREE**. He was once little too and look at him now!"

# THE TREE OF LIFE

A tree was once
A tiny seed
It needed time
To become a tree

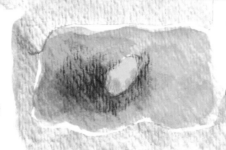

Under the earth
It began to grow
What it would become
It didn't know

In certain ways
We're like a tree
What we will becom[e]
Is for us to see

It just kept...
GROWING and GROWING and GROWING and
Popped out of the soil one day

Nothing could stop it
It kept moving upward
No matter what stood in the way

Each one of us
Is here to grow
There's much to lear[n]
And a lot to know

Its leaves sprouted out and
Its stalk and branches
Climbed upward and reached to the sky

Nurtured by sun and the rain
The small seed never dreamed
It would grow so very high

## Chorus

Just keep...
DOING and DOING and DOING and DOING
The best you can do every day

Believe in yourself
Take one step at a time
Don't let anything stand in your way

When you're least expecting it someone will lend you a hand
When you reach out to each other and help one another
That makes life so very grand

But if things are going wrong
And they aren't the way they should be
When you're feeling bad or sad

Think of a beautiful tree
How it grows majestically
Towards the rain and sun up above

Keep hope in your heart
Right from the start
And nurture each other with love

Repeat Chorus

Hailey and Logan woke up from their magical dream.
The rain had stopped and the sun was shining. They continued
walking home.

"Hailey, look at the flowers coming up!" shouted Logan.
"Let's pick some for Mommy."

The children looked up at the sky and with wonder, saw a glorious
rainbow shining above.

# Acknowledgments

## My heartfelt thank you to…

My son and daughter-in-law David and Alejandra, for your enormous help in creating the files for the books and songs as well as your wonderful design input.
The love and support from both of you and Joe, my life partner, have been so meaningful and encouraging to me.

My nieces and nephews, Gillian, Hailey, Joshua, Isaac, and Logan, for being my inspiration in creating memorable characters for the books.
My brother-in-law, Michael Getlan, for your untiring motivation to have the books published. You and Laurie have been instrumental in "getting the message out!"

My sister-in-law, Ellen Seader, reading specialist, and her mother, Erna Chaut, former Dean of the School of Education, Adelphi University. Your assistance with editing have been invaluable. The love and encouragement from you, my niece Jamie Lippiner, and sister-in-laws Joan Seader and Diane Seader, have been a tremendous help to me.

My friends and family, for your enthusiasm, suggestions, and contributions.
Sally Smollar and Peggy Gorman-children's librarians, Robert Boyar- marketing consultant, Stephanie Goldreyer and Sondra Levine- editing, Cumi Villagran- for converting the files to PowerPoint and to Joanne Schadler- graphic designer, for creating this page.

My graphic designers at Venture Promotions - Dice Garcia and Yelena Mudretsova, as well as at Searles Graphics - Rob Seifert and Nicole Jakob. You have done an exceptional job preparing the files for print. I truly appreciate your patience and expertise.
My book manufacturer, Color House Graphics, the outstanding company I have chosen. I want to especially thank Sandy Gould for making the experience so pleasant.

My talented musician, Larry Sachetillo, for your musical arrangements and instrumentation that have enlivened the songs with your wonderful spirit.
My Aunt Gloria Stroock, actress, and Uncle Leonard Stern, writer, producer, publisher, for your guidance and for sharing with us your seasoned wisdom and expertise.

I am forever grateful to my sister Valerie for her exceptional work illustrating and co-creating the book series with me.
It will be a joy to continue working together to complete our goal…
the **In Your Heart Lives a Rainbow** series of 7 books.

CD of 11 songs for the first three books is included in Book 1.

The same CD is also available inside the case above.
It can be purchased on our website:

**InYourHeartLivesaRainbow.com**